Malaika's First Rainbow Adventure

To our dearest Malaika – know that you are wise, brave, loving and beautiful. Thank you for all that you have taught us. Love from Mummy and Daddy

To all of the rainbow children on the Earth:

Work Your Magic!

Published in association with Bear With Us Productions

©2021 Mili Wright
The right of Mili Wright as the author of this work has been asserted by her in accordance with the Copyright Designs and Patents Act 1988.

Malaika's First Rainbow Adventure

WRITTEN BY MILI WRIGHT

ILLUSTRATED BY OANA GHEORGHE

BEAR W!TH US PRODUCTIONS

Once upon a rainbow

there lived a little girl called Malaika.

She lived in a **rainbow** house and she played in a **rainbow** garden.

One colourful and sunny day, her wizarding guide came to visit.

Malaika and the wizard sat in the garden and talked, whilst enjoying **rainbow** juice and **rainbow** cookies.

"I have a challenging mission for you to complete," said the wizard. Malaika's eyes lit up.

"Oh, I love an adventure!" she cheered with excitement.

"Yes, an adventure is a good way to look at it," replied the wizard, smiling. "It will take place tomorrow and you will need some tools." The wizard handed Malaika a sparkly bag.

Malaika emptied the contents onto the table and out fell:

some small stones,

a box with "loud voice" written on it,

a red nose

and some balloons.

"I'll be on my way now," said the wizard, walking towards the rainbow gate.

"But how will I know where to go or what my mission is or how to use these?" Malaika asked, looking at the objects on the table.

"You'll know, follow your intuition," the wizard said. "And one more piece of advice, remember to think with your heart when you come across any problems that might need solving."

The next day, Malaika set off with her sparkly bag of tools and delicious rainbow sandwiches, and slid down the beautiful rainbow.

Soon, she came across a river.
She approached the shallow
part of it and saw a bunny
rabbit hopping around looking
very scared.

"Are you feeling OK?"
asked Malaika.

What if......?
I can't!

The bunny looked at her with wide eyes and blurted out,

"My tummy feels like it is full of fluttering butterflies and my mind keeps saying 'I can't!' and 'what if...'! I can't swim you see, and what if I get swept away by the river? It's all too much for me to cope with and I just want to run away or hide, but I also want to cross the river."

"That's fear," replied Malaika. "It's good to have some fear, but it shouldn't stop you from doing what you want to do. Let's solve the problem."

Malaika took the stones from her bag and shouted,

"GROW!"

The stones landed in the river and grew to create stepping stones.

"Come with me." Malaika encouraged the bunny. "One day I will teach you to swim, but for now let's cross the river together. And remember, no more what ifs or I can'ts!"

Malaika and Bunny hopped across the stepping stones and reached the other side. The bunny stayed with Malaika and they continued the journey together.

A few hours later, they came to a park where they saw an angry, big boy bullying some smaller children and taking their lunches.

"Oh dear," babbled Bunny, "what if he bullies us and takes your rainbow sandwiches?"

"Remember, no more what ifs," Malaika said to Bunny, sternly.

Malaika reached into her bag and pulled out the box with "loud voice" written on it. She opened it and pointed it at the children and adults who were watching.

Stop that!

They all started walking towards the bully and they began to speak up. The bully stopped, became very embarrassed and started to cry.

Malaika and Bunny walked towards the bully.

"What is the matter? Why are you crying?" asked Malaika, speaking confidently.

"I feel like I don't belong. I need to be in control because it's easier for me to understand what is going on around me," sobbed the bully. "I feel alone at home and at school."

"Well!" exclaimed Malaika. "Come with us! We will be your friends and I am sure you will find some more on the way."

"Remember," Malaika said to the boy, "it is OK to be angry, but it is not OK to be unkind to others. Anger tries to step in and protect us if we are feeling helpless, scared, threatened, hurt, fed up or out of control."

"It is a reaction more than it is an emotion. We could even call anger a 'cover emotion'. Anger can also help us move forward in a positive way, but you must never bully others."

The boy nodded and Malaika, Bunny and the boy continued their walk.

After stopping for some **rainbow** sandwiches, they came across a children's hospital.

The three of them walked in and saw many children who were unwell and sad. Some were crying and some were in pain.

"We try our best to cheer them up," said the nurses and doctors,

"but they could definitely do with some more happiness."

"I know!" exclaimed Malaika with a big grin on her face. She reached into her sparkly bag and took out her red nose and balloons.

Bunny, the boy and Malaika became funny, silly clowns and made balloon models for each child.

Soon it was time to go home.
"I'm staying," said the boy. "I have
made lots of friends here and I will
continue to cheer them up! I am going
to be a play leader!"

So, Bunny and Malaika said their goodbyes and headed home. When they reached the river, Bunny hopped across the stones happily without any what ifs or I can'ts. Malaika said goodbye and returned to her rainbow house.

One colourful and sunny morning, the wizard came back.

"Well done, Malaika! You have completed your mission – you thought with your heart and you were very resilient throughout."

The wizard handed her a golden star.

"Here you go, this is your prize and something you can use on your next adventure."

He pinned the star to her dress, gave her a smile and a wink and headed out through the

rainbow garden gate.

Malaika admired the star and wondered what her next mission would be.

Thank you!

- To the hospital staff who do such a wonderful job including the play specialists and Simon for your balloon modelling and cheering up all the children

- To every child I have worked with during my time in education, you have all helped me to create this book

- To all of you who buy this book and use it to bring awareness to our children

- To my wonderful husband, Shaun, who supports me with all of my creative endeavours!

About the author

Mili Wright grew up in Oxfordshire, in a town called Bicester. She has worked with children for most of her life and now specialises in special educational needs in mainstream schools. Mili also works as a spiritual intuitive coach and a Reiki Master. As a healer and an educator, she believes that having a deep awareness of our emotions will give us the knowledge that we need to live in a peaceful world. Her daughter, the children she has worked with and her passion for emotional literacy, have inspired her to write this book.

Message from the author:

"Nurturing and understanding your emotions can help you to have a greater awareness of self and others. By understanding each other and ourselves, we can create a compassionate and peaceful world."

—Mili Wright

Ideas on how to use this book for teachers and parents

Activities:

1. Discuss each emotion in the book and when children may have experienced them

2. Discuss where emotions can be felt in the body and label them to aid with self-awareness

3. Create emotion potions with food colouring, water and glitter

4. Create emotion potion antidotes e.g., if you are feeling fear, you may need a potion made of trust

5. Create emotion poems linking to personification

6. Create emotion characters

7. Map out and identify where the primary emotions (fear, anger, sadness and happiness) occur in the book

8. What does the wizarding guide mean by advising Malaika to think with her heart? Discuss the importance of compassion and when we might be compassionate to others

9. Explore when children have felt angry. Was there an underlying feeling before they felt angry? How can we show love and care towards the underlying emotion that is being covered up?

10. Write down how you feel when you are angry. Does this help to understand what is going on?

11. Explore moving the anger through the body to let it go in a positive way e.g., artwork, shouting into a pillow, going for a run

12. Create inner-coach cards e.g., "With focus and determination I can..."

13. Each child can create their own tools and magic bag to help them with emotions that they find challenging

14. Create personal affirmations and affirmations for characters in the story e.g., 'I am brave', 'You can do it!'

15. Explore negative thoughts and flip them into positive thoughts. Create a success thought poster or bookmark to refer to throughout the day or before bedtime